This book is presented
by
First Lady Christie Vilsack
on behalf of
Iowa Stories 2000

This book belongs to:

Thanks to our sponsors:

IOWA AEA AREA EDUCATION AGENCIES

WELLS FARGO HOME MORTGAGE

PATTEE

IOWA FARM BUREAU

Sigler Companies
Innova Ideas & Services • Sigler Printing & Publishing
McMillen Publishing • United Fulfillment Solutions

verizon
Make progress every day

HyVee
EMPLOYEE OWNED

David and Liz Kruidenier

The Des Moines Register
Full of Life
DesMoinesRegister.com

ROTARY INTERNATIONAL
District 6000 Rotary

Anne and Bill Riley

CASEY'S GENERAL STORE

BLUE BUNNY
Wells

OAKS DEVELOPMENT COMPANY
Quietly Iowa's Largest

McAninch

Cookies

MAYTAG
CORPORATION

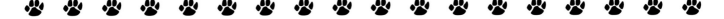

Bells Goes to the Fair

Written by Susan Knapp

Illustrated by
John Whitehurst

Photographs by
Susan Knapp

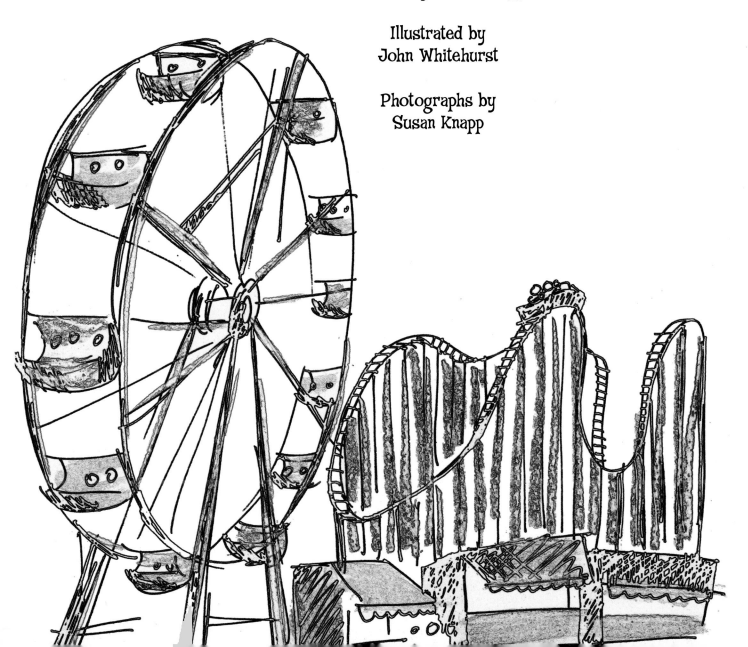

Bells Goes to the Fair

Published by Susan Knapp
5000 Westown Parkway, Suite 100
West Des Moines, IA 50266
515-223-4000
knappprop@aol.com

Publishing Manager: Denise Sundvold

Printed and distributed by:

McMillen Publishing
A Sigler Company
413 Northwestern
Ames, Iowa 50010
515-232-0208
www.mcmillenbooks.com

Designed by Erin R. Borcherding

Library of Congress Control Number: 2002109110

ISBN 1-888-223-49-9

FOREWORD

Bells Goes to the Fair was inspired in 1997. One evening while our family and a few guests were having dinner at our campsite at the Iowa State Fair, we discovered that Bells had gotten loose from her leash. She was lost for a couple of hours. During that time Bells visited several different barns. The Livestock Control officers helped in finding and returning Bells to our family, safe and sound.

ACKNOWLEDGEMENTS

The writing of this book has been a family affair. Many thanks to my extended family in Santa Barbara, California, who helped develop the illustrations for this book: Mark Whitehurst and Kerry Methner, who assisted with the digital art from photographs that I shot while at the fair; and John Whitehurst, who developed the Bells caricature. A special thank you to Mark Whitehurst, who suggested the dual readership which enabled us to expand our reader audience. Thanks also to Lois Braby and Suzan Kelsey Brooks, who edited the book. Thanks to Joyce Lock, my fair buddy, who planted the seed for Bells Goes To The Fair. Finally, I would like to say thank you to my husband, Bill, for his help in making this book possible.

—Susan Knapp

Story written in larger text for a short story. Ages 1-5.

Story written in smaller text for a more detailed look at Bells' adventure.

Ages 6 and up.

Everyone has been busy for days packing the motor home with all kinds of fun and interesting things.

Whenever the family starts to load the motor home, Bells is on the lookout for clues that she may be going along. She notices that the last things to be packed were her ball, her food and her water dish. Those are good signs!

Anna cries, "Come Bells, come. We're going to the fair!"

Bells bounds into the motor home and everyone is off to the Iowa State Fair. Now, this fair is the best state fair in the whole wide world! Sara's favorite thing is to ride the double ferris wheel in the midway. Anna loves to bake and try to win a Blue Ribbon for the best cookies at the fair.

Packing the motor home is how it
all begins. We load fun things like the tent,
checkers and bubble gum.

Sometimes things roll out of the cupboards on the way to the Iowa State Fair.

Sara and Anna's stepdad, Bill, drives the motor home while their mom, Susan, is busy making sure nothing rolls out of the cupboards or onto the floors. She is also busy making sure that Bill takes the right roads to Des Moines where the famous Iowa State Fair is held every year. Sara and Anna are playing a game of checkers. It is important that they practice so that one of them might win the Blue Ribbon in the checkers contest!

Anna says, "Bells, we're here! We're here! We're here at the fair!"

Bells already seems to know they're at the fair because she can smell the familiar scents of the wonderful "fair food"...corn dogs, cotton candy, kettle corn, dip-n-dots, tenderloins and even the lemonade. Everything smells so-o-o-o good! Bells loves to walk through the fair with Sara and Anna because she gets to see all of the barns. How she wishes that someday she could go inside and visit with the animals!

Bill pulls the motor home into the campsite, and the family unloads. They put Bells on her leash.

Smells, wonderful smells, at the fair. Bells already knows she has arrived. Everything smells so-o-o-o good!

Sara says, "Bells, you'll be safe here while we unload the motor home."

The family sets up their lawn chairs and the picnic table and puts up the awning on the motor home. The campsite will be their "home away from home" for the next ten days. After everything is in order, they're ready to see what's happening at the fair. But before they leave the campsite, Anna says, "Sara, will you get the bubble gum out of the camper so we can practice our bubble blowing skit for the 4-H Share the Fun Contest? I want to win a Blue Ribbon for our performance this year!"

Sara gets the gum and gives Anna her pieces.

**Blowing as big a bubble as you can is fun.
Sara and Anna blow and blow and blow and
hope the bubble doesn't pop!**

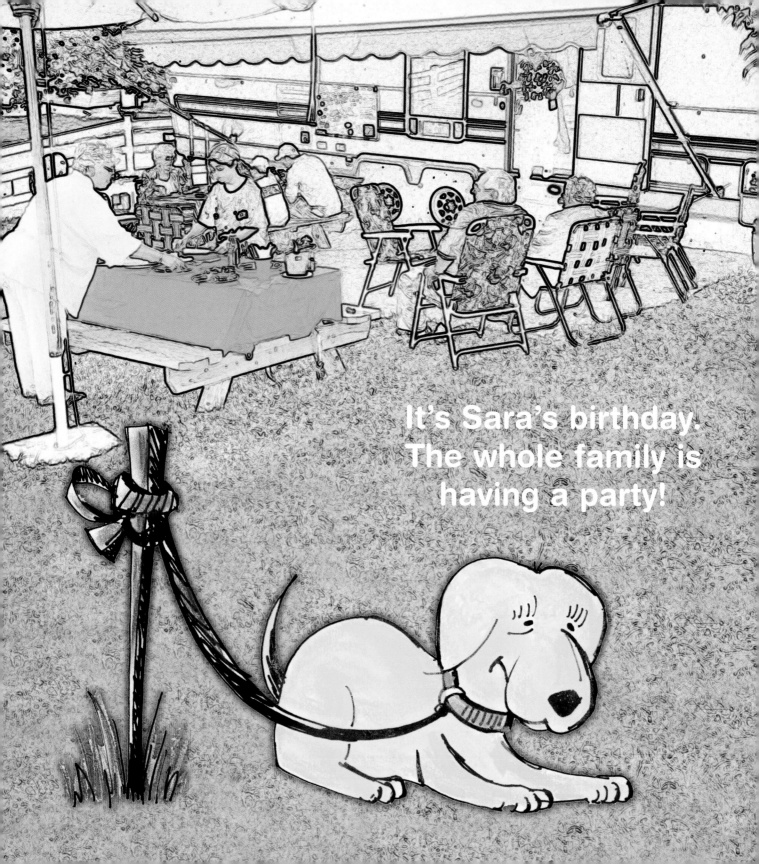

It's Sara's birthday. The whole family is having a party!

Today is Sara's birthday, and everyone is singing "Happy Birthday to Sara," when Bells suddenly realizes that she is free from her leash!

Because everyone is so busy enjoying Sara's birthday party, Bells decides this would be the perfect time to visit all those interesting animals in the fairground barns.

Bells finds she is free.
She heads straight for the animal barns.
She wants to make some new friends.

The first barn that Bells spots is the poultry barn. She thinks, "This should be interesting. I guess I'll just stroll in." There Bells finds chickens...endless cages of chickens. At least fifty different kinds. It's so exciting that she decides to find out what's happening here.

She walks up to a Banty Rooster. "Chicken," Bells says, "there are so many of you, and you're all so beautiful! What in the world are you doing here?"

The Banty Rooster answers with a big smile, "We're here to win a Blue Ribbon! Look around you and you might notice that we chickens actually resemble people. Maybe even a few you would recognize. There's even one that looks like Britney Spears! Take a look and see what you think."

Bells looks at all the chickens and answers, "Sure enough, Banty Rooster, that chicken looks just like her, and there's one that looks like Dolly Parton. And over there is one that sure reminds me of Willie Nelson. Chickens that look like stars...wow...this is fun!"

Bells makes friends with Banty Rooster right away. Chickens love to fluff up their feathers and strut.

Bells turns and heads for the rabbits. As she comes closer, she sees hundreds and hundreds of different-colored and strange-looking rabbits. Bells thinks, "I have never seen rabbits like this in my barnyard!"

Bells sniffs at the large rabbit in the Blue Ribbon cage. Bells nudges him on the nose and asks, "Rabbit, you're way too big for me to chase! What in the world are you doing here at the Iowa State Fair?"

The rabbit smiles and answers proudly with his nose high in the air, "I am the biggest and best rabbit of the whole fair! You may call me King of the Hares. I am even big enough to chase you!"

With that, Bells turns on her heels and runs as fast as she can away from the "King of Hares!"

The biggest rabbit at the fair tells Bells,
"I am King of the Hares!
I am so big I can chase you!"

Soon Bells finds her way to the cattle barn. She sees a huge Black Angus steer who is being groomed for the show ring. The steer is in the process of having his coat blown dry by his groomer when Bells steps close to him and asks, "Steer, what in the world are they doing to you?"

The steer looks over at Bells and answers with a bit of pride, "I am being made ready for the Governor's Charity Steer Show in the Livestock Pavilion. I am hoping to win a Blue Ribbon for the Best of Show steer. Wish me luck, will you?"

Bells answers with a nod of her head. "Good luck steer! You look very fine!"

"Wow! This is great!" Bells thinks to herself.

Bells wants to see the cattle barn where all the cows stay. Everything along the way looks and smells so-o-o-o good!

Bells is headed toward the Jersey cows who are being milked by a milking machine. The Dairy Barn takes the fresh milk from the Jersey cows and turns it into fresh ice cream. Bells is delighted when she finds a pistachio flavored ice cream cone on the ground. "Yummy!" says Bells. "I love fair food."

Bells scoops up
a green ice cream
cone from off the
sidewalk and
gobbles it down.
"Yummy! I love fair food."

But, suddenly, she hears a very loud snort and finds herself eyeball-to-eyeball with the "Biggest Bull" at the fair! Bells has never seen anything so big in her whole life. The sign says "This bull weighs 3,000 pounds."

"Holy cow!" Bells thinks to herself. "I'm glad this guy is in that stall and can't chase me!"

Bells hears a loud snort.
She turns around, and
there is a HUGE bull.
"Yikes!" Bells is scared.

Suddenly, back at the campsite, Mom says to Dad, "Where in the world is Bells?"

Then everyone begins to search for Bells. They immediately head for the fairgrounds. Sara, Anna, Mom and Dad split up and go in different directions. The fairgrounds are very large, with a lot of territory to cover. And if they are going to find Bells before dark, they must hurry!

Sara finds a Livestock Control Officer. She asks, "Excuse me, sir, but we've lost our dog! Have you seen a yellow lab come this way?"

"Yes," replies the officer, "I saw her about an hour ago. She was walking out of the poultry barn and heading toward the cattle barn."

"Thank you very much!" Sara yells over her shoulder as she takes off running toward the cattle barn.

Meanwhile Bells comes upon three sheep that are being sheared. "Oh my goodness," Bells says to one of the sheep. "What in the world are they doing, undressing you?!"

The sheep responds, "These people are in a contest to see who can shear our wool the fastest. The fastest one will win the Blue Ribbon. Don't worry, it really feels good to shed this bunch of wool. It's a pretty hot summer, you know!"

Bells is at the sheep barn. People are shaving wool off the sheep.

Anna walks outside and, luckily, finds a Livestock Control Officer. She asks, "Have you seen a yellow lab? We've lost our dog!"

The officer responds, "I saw a yellow lab leaving the cattle barn and heading for the sheep barn about thirty minutes ago. That's probably your dog."

Anna yells, "Thank you, Officer," then darts toward the sheep barn.

Anna is searching for Bells. She is afraid they will not find her before dark.

After leaving the sheep barn, Bells heads for the swine barn. On the way, however, she sees a corn dog lying on a bench. She thinks as she snatches it up and swallows it, "Yummy! That's the best thing I have ever eaten...I do love fair food!"

"Yummy!" Bells gets her first taste of a corn dog. She loves fair food!

As Bells enters the swine barn, the first thing she sees is a farrowing display of baby pigs. She walks up to the mama pig who is nursing her babies.

"Pig," says Bells, "your baby pigs are really hungry!"

The mama pig responds, "I'm a sow and I've just given birth to five piglets. What do you think of that?! They're only a couple of hours old. Now, I would stop to chat, but I am really quite tired. So if you wouldn't mind, I'd like to take a nap!"

"I sure don't mind. It looks like you have a reason to be tired with such a group of piglets around you!" Bells didn't know that pigs could be so small.

The mama pig has five new baby piglets.
Bells stares at them and wishes she could
give them each a kiss.

After a while, Bells makes her way out of the swine barn and heads for the horse barn. Suddenly, she comes upon the Bill Riley Stage show. Boys and girls are singing their special songs in hopes of winning a Blue Ribbon. Bells decides to join in. Bells loves to sing. When she has finished her special "howling" song, everyone claps for her performance! She hopes she might win a Blue Ribbon, too! However, that just wasn't meant to be.

Kids are singing and Bells has to join in. She sings and sings. Everyone claps as they hear her song.

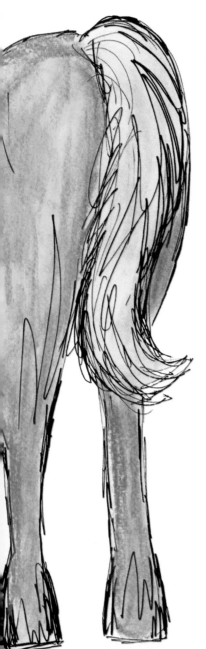

On the way to the horses, Bells spots a tasty-looking funnel cake covered with powdered sugar frosting, just lying there on the ground. She gobbles it right down. Bells stomach is starting to feel just a little bit "woozy" by now. All this "people fair food" isn't setting so well with her dog stomach. But she goes along.

Once inside the horse barn, Bells comes upon the HUGE draft horses! All of them are quite friendly to Bells. They seem to like it when she sniffs at them and really want to stay and play with Bells, but they have to get suited up to pull their shiny wagons at the Livestock Pavilion. They all want to win a Blue Ribbon for being the best draft team at the fair! So, Bells once more says, "Goodbye," to her new-found friends and leaves for her next adventure.

Near the horse barn, Bells looks curiously as the big horse looks down on her. But Bells is not afraid. She is making a new friend.

Bells leads the way as the horse team trots to the horse show.

Walking along, Bells spots a giant slide. She walks over, thinking that she might just try it. But a voice shouts, "Hey, you can't go up there! That's just for kids and people...not animals!"

While the man is busy taking tickets, Bells sneaks up the steps to take a ride on the big slide. And slide she does! She jumps on a canvas rug that is at the top of the steps, then shouts with gusto, "Wheeeeeeeeeeeeeee!" all the way down! It is such fun!

Bells sneaks up the long stairs so she can ride down the Giant Slide. "Wheeeeeee!"

But when she gets off the slide, Bells asks herself, "Golly...where am I? Where will I go?"

It's getting dark, and Bells has lost her way. She looks in all the barns wondering which is the way back to Sara and Anna and the campsite?

Suddenly Bells realizes she is lost.
How is she ever going to find her way back
to Sara and Anna at the campsite?

Suddenly, Bells is surrounded by three horses. She looks up and sees, smiling down on her, three people who are calling her by name. They are the friendly Livestock Control Officers, so Bells is not afraid when one jumps off his horse and snatches her up in his arms. He and Bells hop back on his horse, and he says, "You've given your owners a big scare! They thought you were lost for good. I'll take you home now."

Bells looks up and sees three riders on horses. One scoops Bells up and takes her to her fair home.

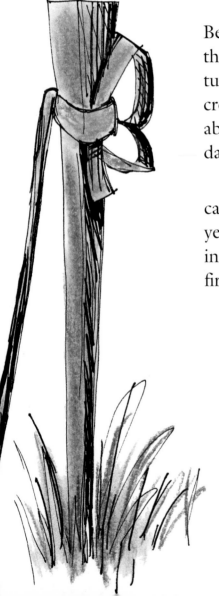

Bells sleeps quite soundly that night except for the occasional growling sounds from her tummy, for she had filled it with corn dog, ice cream and funnel cake! She dreams all night about the many animal friends she made that day in their different barns.

Bells will return to the fair and stay at the campsite with Sara and Anna next year and the year after that and the year after that, but nothing will ever be as exciting to Bells as her very first day at the fair!

Bells is glad to be back at the camper.
She falls fast asleep!

The End